Reading Esse
in Socia

MW00825277

AMERICA IN THE 1800s

Courage on the Oregon Trail

Dorothy Francis

PERFECTION LEARNING®

Editorial Director: Susan C. Thies
Editor: Mary L. Bush

Cover Design: Michael A. Aspengren
Book Design: Emily J. Greazel, Deborah Lea Bell
Image Research: Lisa Lorimor

Photo Credits:
© North Wind Pictures: pp. 4–5 (top), 18; © Denver Public Library Western
History Department: pp. 13 (top), 16, 16–17, 18–19, 19, 20–21, 22, 28–29,
30 (bottom), 30–31, 37; © Nebraska State Historical Society, Lincoln:
pp. 12–13 (bottom); © Solomon D. Butcher Collection Nebraska State
Historical Society: pp. 10–11; © Kansas State Historical Society: p. 14

ArtToday (some images copyright www.arttoday.com): cover (bottom-center),
pp. 2–3 (center), 3 (bottom), 4–5 (bottom), 6 (background), 6–7, 27, 32; Corel
Professional Photos: cover, pp. 1, 2–3 (top and bottom), 6, 23, 30 (top), 35, 36,
38–39; Library of Congress: pp. 9, 33, 34

For information, contact
Perfection Learning® Corporation
1000 North Second Avenue, P.O. Box 500
Logan, Iowa 51546-0500.
Phone: 1-800-831-4190
Fax: 1-800-543-2745
perfectionlearning.com

3 4 5 6 7 PP 09 08 07 06 05

Paperback ISBN 0-7891-5872-8

Reinforced Library Binding ISBN 0-7569-4487-2

Contents

Wagon-wheel ruts cut into the stone along the Oregon Trail still exist today.

The Oregon Trail extended from the banks of the Missouri River to the Oregon prairie.

Chapter 1

Thief on Horseback

Luke heard the thumping of Ruthie's shoes. They were wearing thin, and the soles were flapping as she walked.

The Fletchers had walked beside their covered wagon for a month. Now they were deep into Nebraska. Fort Kearney lay two days behind them.

Ruthie yanked off her shoes. She threw them into the tall prairie grass.

"What are you going to do now?" Luke asked.

"Go barefoot," Ruthie said. "June is barefoot time."

"Jumpin' horned toads, Ruthie," Luke said. "It's a long way to Oregon. Fetch the shoes and tie 'em back on."

"You're not my boss," Ruthie said. "My feet hurt. I'm done with shoes." Ruthie's dark eyes flashed. Anger flushed her face clear to her dark bangs.

Luke sighed. Ten-year-old Ruthie looked a lot like Pa. But unlike Pa, she often acted silly. She needed a brother's advice. After all, he was two years older than she was. He knew so much more than she did. But Ruthie got mad as a wasp in a bottle if he mentioned that.

"Want knife."

The deep voice startled them. They hadn't heard anybody approach. Ruthie ran to the other side of the wagon.

Luke looked up at the Indian riding a skinny **Appaloosa**. Green paint smeared his face. Black spiky hair bristled down the middle of his bald head. Bones and teeth circled his neck on a **thong**.

The hair on Luke's nape stiffened. His heart pounded like a **tom-tom**.

A few Native Americans tried to force the pioneers off the prairie, which had been their home for thousands of years. The majority of Native Americans, however, were friendly to travelers along the trail.

"Want knife," the Indian repeated. He rode close and raised a club.

Luke could smell the sweat of the tired horse. He pulled the hunting knife from his belt and handed it to the Indian. The coppery taste of fear coated Luke's tongue. He held his breath.

The thief kicked his pony and cantered away. Luke breathed again.

Now the family came running. Jake, the wagon master, joined them. He sat astride Hawkeye, his **buckskin** stallion.

"Oh, Luke!" Ma shouted and rushed to hug him. Luke tried not to squirm. Ever since Mark had died, Ma hugged him a lot.

Pa patted Luke's shoulder, his brown eyes dark with concern. Ruthie clung to Ma's **calico** skirt.

Jake towered over everyone when he dismounted. A wide-brimmed hat shaded his weathered face. His flint-gray eyes bore into Luke.

"Are you hurt?" Jake asked.

"N—no," Luke said. "But he took my knife—the knife my brother made. Mark carved my initials on the walnut handle." Luke wished he'd been braver. Why hadn't he fought for the knife?

Why hadn't he fought to save Mark from the fire? Because you're a coward, inner voices accused.

"You're lucky you only lost a knife, boy!" Jake said. "Peter Lee said Indians killed an **emigrant** last month. They scalped him and took his horse. Then they just rode away. Now I guard Peter Lee's leather bag when he's out **scouting**."

"What's in it?" Ruthie asked.

"Peter Lee doesn't say," Jake said. "And I don't pry."

Ruthie stopped asking questions.

Luke liked Peter Lee, the **wagon train's** scout. Peter Lee told great tales about escaping from his slave master and his life as a fur trapper.

"Peter Lee knows Indian ways," Jake said. "He also knows the trails through this wild country. I listen to his advice."

"Peter Lee says many Indians are friendly," Pa said. "They often help repair wagons. Sometimes they show emigrants where to find wild **game**."

"Yes," Jake agreed. "You did right, Luke. It's smart to be friendly with the Indians."

But Luke knew that he'd acted in fear, not because he was smart. He was good at acting in fear. Memories of their house fire haunted him. He could still feel himself choking on black smoke.

Luke had jumped from a window. Juniper bushes had softened his fall. Then his parents and sister had escaped down the stairs. But the roof had collapsed before his brother could get out. Mark had died trapped upstairs. March 5, 1859—Luke would always remember that date.

Why hadn't he stayed with Mark? Luke asked himself all the time.

Pa said Luke couldn't have helped. But inner voices shouted *coward*!

Now, two months later, he'd given up Mark's knife. Once again, he'd been a coward.

Luke knew why Pa had decided to move west. Jobs were scarce, so many emigrants moved to earn a better living. But Pa had made a good living farming. He had decided to make the journey to start a new life for the family.

Living in Missouri without Mark had made their hearts hurt. Perhaps a new life in Oregon would ease some of the pain.

It was a custom among some Native American tribes to exchange gifts with strangers. Pioneers who knew this often received needed food and supplies as well as helpful advice.

Chapter 2

Emigrants or Pioneers?

Pa said that *emigrants* were people who moved to a **foreign** country. Ma said that people who settled new lands were called *pioneers.*

Oregon had just become a state last month. So now it wasn't a foreign country. Does that make us emigrants or pioneers? Luke wondered.

Either way, they did a heap of walking. Oregon may be in the United States, but it was sure a long way from Missouri.

The Fletchers had packed everything they owned into their **prairie schooner**. The blue and white cover would help keep things dry. Ruthie had helped Luke paint the wheels red.

The oxen had been named for their ear colors—Purple, Green, Yellow, and Red. Luke had begged to save the critters from the **branding iron**. He'd boiled leaves and berries to make colored dyes to mark the oxen instead.

The wagon held their tent, tools, and food. Luke had packed up Pa's hammer, saws, pliers, jacks, crowbars, and screwdrivers. Ruthie's mouth had watered as she piled in beans, bacon, grain, salt, coffee, and dried fruits. Ma packed eggs in flour to keep them from breaking.

Pioneers packed as many of their belongings as their wagon could carry. The rest had to be left behind.

Pa had added a tiny carpet, one chair, a box of china, and a mirror. Ma cried when she left behind their grandfather clock and the **four-poster bed**.

Luke and Ruthie had each picked a few of their special things to take with them. The rest was left behind.

"Platte River up ahead!" Jake shouted. "Steep slope. Rope the wagons."

Luke quickly forgot about Missouri as they approached the river.

Pa slowed their oxen. Luke ran to the edge of a bluff and looked down. Sunshine glinted on the river. Water gurgled over brown rocks and under willows.

"At last!" Luke called to Ruthie. "Something different."

They helped Pa unhitch the oxen. Each one led a critter down the **bank**. Dirt and rock flew from under the oxen's feet.

Luke gasped when he fell. He slid down the bank on the seat of his pants. But he held tight to the lead rope. Digging in his heels, he slowed himself.

"Come and guard the oxen while they drink," Pa ordered Luke and Ruthie.

Ruthie stayed near Purple and Yellow. Luke watched Red and Green. The oxen gulped and slurped. They drank as if they were filling hollow barrels.

Luke flopped on this stomach and drank too. He squished icy water around in his mouth until his teeth tingled. What a great feeling! Some folks said **cholera** came from drinking river water. But no one on their train had been sick yet.

Then the real excitement began. Up on the trail, men had attached ropes to the wagons. Pa allowed Luke to help the men lower their rigs. Down. Down. Luke felt the rope tighten around

his wrist. The wagon must weigh a ton or more, he thought.

The rope burned Luke's hands, but he held on. He hoped Ruthie was watching. The wagon creaked and groaned. His breath snagged in his throat. What if their wagon tipped over? What if someone broke a leg?

At last their wagon rested beside the river. Luke flopped down and panted for breath. He hoped Ruthie didn't notice that.

After many hours, all the wagons sat beside the river. Luke joined in when everyone cheered.

"We'll stay here overnight!" Jake shouted. "We've earned our rest today."

Again, Luke felt proud. Pa let him help center their wagon **tongue** under the wagon ahead. That was a man's job. And, yes, Ruthie was watching.

Ruthie kept a close eye on the forty-eight wagons as they formed two circles. The wagon rings provided a safe place for the oxen to graze. Sometimes they also protected the camp from Indians or wild animals.

These wagon train rings formed near Independence Rock, Devils Gate, and the Sweetwater River.

Buffalo chips provided fuel for warming homes, heating water, and cooking on the prairie.

When he finished with the wagon, Luke said, "Your turn to gather buffalo **dung**, Ruthie."

"You're not my boss," Ruthie said.

"I did it yesterday," Luke said. "Choose dry chips. Damp dung makes a smoky fire."

Ruthie groaned. "What's your chore?" she asked.

"I'm fetching water," Luke said.

Luke had expected excitement on this trip. But until today, the trail had offered nothing but treeless prairie and endless walking. They rose at sunrise, ate breakfast, and packed up the camp. By 8 a.m., they were back on the trail. Two miles an hour was a good speed for the oxen, but it was a long, boring walk for the people.

Today had been different though. Luke thought about his stolen knife and roping the wagons. Today had given him plenty of excitement!

It had also left him sleepy. After supper, Luke helped Pa raise their tent. Then he dropped onto his blanket and slept.

During the night, a snorting sound wakened him. Then he heard a rasping noise. Indians? Wolves? Shivering, Luke crawled from the tent. All he saw were dying campfires.

Then the sound came again.

Chapter 3

The Humming Box

Luke didn't dare wake Pa. He needed his rest. So did Ma. Ruthie wouldn't be any help. What should he do?

He smelled the dying dung embers and shivered from the cold. Or was it from fear? No, Luke decided. He wouldn't give in to his fear. This was his chance to be brave.

Crawling on his hands and knees, Luke crept under their wagon. The night was as black as the inside of a chimney. The snorting-rasping noise continued. Standing, Luke eased along the circled wagons. Suddenly he stumbled over something.

Luke looked down. It was a leg! A man lay asleep on the ground in front of him. He was snoring loudly. That was the snorting-rasping sound! So much for Indians or wolves, Luke thought.

He could make out a rifle on the man's lap. Jake had promised to post night guards to protect the wagons. Some guard this fellow was!

Luke started to shake the man's leg. But what if the shaking scared the man into shooting? Luke dropped down beside the man, deciding to let him sleep. He could shout for help if danger appeared.

His eyes burned, and he yawned frequently. Exhausted, Luke watched for wolves and Indians until sunrise. He jumped up when Peter Lee approached carrying his leather bag.

15

Women on the trail had many jobs—cooking, washing clothes, chopping wood, tending animals, and watching the children.

"What are you doing here, boy?" Peter Lee asked.

"Keeping guard," Luke said. He pointed to the sleeping man. "I heard him snoring last night. Thought I'd best not wake him."

Now the sleeper sat up and rubbed his eyes. Just then, Jake appeared riding Hawkeye.

"What's going on here?" Jake asked. "Are you up to mischief, Luke?"

"No mischief," Peter Lee said. "Luke sat guard last night." Peter Lee pointed to the man who was still yawning. "Jeb woke Luke with his snoring."

Jake scowled at the sleepy guard.

"Luke, I'm adding your name to our roster of guards," Jake said. "You'll replace Jeb. You'll take regular turns with the other men. Jeb, get out of my sight. Back to your wagons, men. It's chow time."

Luke could hardly believe it. Jake had just called him a man. He wished Ruthie had been around to hear it.

Luke hurried back to his wagon, but Peter Lee beat him. He told the Fletchers of Luke's bravery. That was better, Luke decided. It didn't seem like bragging when someone else said it.

Ma hugged him as usual. Pa patted his shoulder. Ruthie looked impressed, although she wouldn't admit it.

Luke felt mighty proud. Maybe with practice he could learn to be brave.

After breakfast, they **broke** camp and plodded on toward Fort Laramie. The June sun felt like a warm blanket on Luke's shoulders.

Ruthie kicked trail dust with her bare toes. Then she began humming.

"What's that tune?" Luke asked. "I've never heard it before. Are you making up tunes to help pass the time?"

"I hear the song almost every day," Ruthie said. "It clings in my mind. I wish I knew the words."

"Where do you hear it?" Luke asked.

"You know that wagon behind ours?" Ruthie asked.

"Sure," Luke said. "It belongs to the Smiths from Missouri."

"Since her husband died, Mrs. Smith drives their wagon," Ruthie said. "She's lonely. Sometimes she lets me sit on the driver's seat beside her. That's where I hear the music."

"She sings it?" Luke asked.

"No," Ruthie said. "I hear humming coming from a box behind the driver's seat. When Mrs. Smith turns and taps the box, the humming stops."

"Jumpin' horned toads, Ruthie!" Luke said. "You expect me to believe Mrs. Smith has a box that hums?"

Life along the Oregon Trail was difficult. At the end of each day, emigrants would stop to repair wagons, look for water, find grass for grazing animals, and rest briefly before starting all over the next day.

Chapter 4

Songs and Scissors

"It's the pure truth," Ruthie said. "Follow me. I'll show you."

"No!" Luke cried.

Ruthie ignored him and charged up to the Smiths' wagon. Jake was walking beside the wagon leading Hawkeye.

"Mrs. Smith," Ruthie blurted, "please tell Luke about your magic box that hums tunes."

Jake laughed. "You have some imagination, Ruthie!"

"It's pure truth," Ruthie insisted. "Tell him, Mrs. Smith. Please."

"Now, Ruthie," Mrs. Smith said. "We both know that boxes don't hum."

Mrs. Smith's face flushed. Her embarrassment made Luke wonder if Ruthie had been telling the truth.

"Let's open the box," Luke suggested.

"No," Mrs. Smith said. She pulled a blanket over the box.

"Maybe I'd better take a look," Jake said. "I'm responsible for this wagon train's safety. Please open the box."

Mrs. Smith's neck grew cherry red. She didn't make a move to open the box.

Jake pulled himself onto the wagon seat. Everyone gasped as he opened the box.

A black girl a bit bigger than Ruthie stared up at them. Curly black hair almost covered her brown eyes. She sat up, wide-eyed and frightened.

"Please explain," Jake said.

"I've owned Mazie for years," Mrs. Smith said. "I wanted to sell her back in Missouri, but she begged to come along. She's a good girl, Jake. I need her help. She won't cause any trouble."

Luke couldn't imagine one person selling another.

"Oregon is a state now," Jake said. "It's illegal to bring slaves there."

"I can't abandon her." Mrs. Smith began crying. "I need her help."

Jake mopped his forehead with a handkerchief. "I've never had this problem before."

"I have an idea," Luke said. "Mrs. Smith could free Mazie. If she paid her for working, then she could bring her along."

Mrs. Smith sat speechless. Then she smiled through her tears.

"I guess I have no other choice," she said.

"Maybe Mazie doesn't want to work for you," Jake said.

"But I do," Mazie said. "We love each other. Sneaking into Oregon was my idea."

"Then we'll work out the details," Jake said. "But no more hiding. I want to see you out and about helping Mrs. Smith with chores."

"Thank you," Mrs. Smith said to both Luke and Jake. "You've done us a great favor. We're in your debt."

Luke smiled. He, Luke Fletcher, had helped free a slave. He hurried to tell Peter Lee.

––·––·––·––·––·––·––·––·––

Mazie's appearance on the wagon train surprised the travelers. But they welcomed her singing. At campfire, she taught the words to her tunes "Jacob's Ladder," "Swing Low, Sweet Chariot," and "Let My People Go."

Mazie's songs made the weeks pass quicker. The wagons rumbled past unusual rocky **outcroppings** on the prairie.

They passed Courthouse Rock and nearby Jail Rock. These rock formations stood about 400 feet above the North Platte River. Next along the trail was Chimney Rock, a tall rock column over 300 feet high.

Luke, Ruthie, and Mazie hiked off the trail to carve their names on the landmarks.

The train stopped for a day's rest at Fort Laramie. Luke helped Pa buy supplies inside the fort's **adobe** walls. Loaded with new supplies, the wagons crept on and on.

One night, Peter Lee joined the Fletchers' campfire. He jingled the buckles on his leather bag.

"What's in the bag?" Ruthie asked. She stood on tiptoe trying to see. Mazie peeked too. Luke looked over their shoulders into the bag.

Platte River

"Scissors," he reported. "Razors. Combs. Looks like barber tools to me."

"Right," Peter Lee said. "I'm setting up a barbershop when I reach Oregon. I'm tired of Indian scouting and fur trapping."

"Where'd you learn barbering?" Luke asked.

"On a cotton plantation," Peter Lee said. "I gave many of my people haircuts before I ran off. Then I worked for a fur trader. I saved my money and bought barber tools."

Luke and the girls stared at the shiny new tools.

"Luke, I'll make a deal with you," Peter Lee said.

"What kind of a deal?" Luke asked.

"You talk to every wagon driver," Peter Lee said. "Tell them to come see me if they want a haircut. I'll give them a special rate—only 10 cents. I'll give you half the money."

Luke hesitated. His knees shook when he spoke to strangers. Yet, Peter Lee wanted help. And he wanted to earn money. He hid his fear behind a smile.

Luke set off to talk to the men. After the first few, his voice stopped shaking and the fear disappeared. In the end, a dozen men wanted haircuts.

"Sit down, Luke," Peter Lee said. "I'll demonstrate on you."

Everyone watched. This was scarier than talking to the men! Luke gritted his teeth. Snip. Snip. Snip. He heard the scissors. Snip. Snip. Snip. He felt cold steel against his neck. What if folks laughed?

But nobody laughed. Instead the men argued over who would go next.

That night, Luke tucked 60 cents into his pocket. He dreamed about buying another hunting knife.

Suddenly a scream woke him.

"Pa! Ma!" Luke shouted.

Chapter 5

And the Ground Shook

"Sound an alarm," Luke begged. He yanked a blanket around his shoulders. Inner chills made his teeth chatter.

The wailing continued. Ma and Pa sat up.

"Hush, Luke," Pa said. "Don't wake Ruthie. It's only wolves. They howl on moonlit nights."

The wailing continued.

"If they sneak inside our ring, our oxen . . ." Luke whispered.

"They *sound* close," Pa said. "But they're far away. They're serenading one another in the mountains. Echoes carry the sound close. If they prowl near, our guards will drive them off."

Luke's throat felt stiff as a lead pipe. He could barely swallow. He couldn't remember being so scared—except when their house had burned. He lay back down. Hours passed before he dozed again.

The next morning, Luke's breath etched white clouds in the air. He and Ruthie walked behind their wagon. The high canvas cover broke the wind.

Ruthie spotted the dark leather pinned on the wagon cover first. She grabbed Luke's hand and pointed.

"Jumpin' horned toads!" Luke shouted. "Moccasins!" He grabbed the two pairs of leather shoes. Beneath them hung a necklace of bones and teeth.

"That's the Indian's necklace!" Ruthie said.

They slipped the moccasins on. They were warm and comfortable.

"Maybe he rode a long way to say thank you," Luke said.

"Maybe he knew the mountain air would freeze our feet," Ruthie said.

"I'd rather have Mark's knife back," Luke said. But he welcomed the moccasins' soft warmth.

He yanked the necklace off the cover and studied the bones and teeth. Slipping the necklace into his pants pocket, he grinned. Some souvenir! He'd show it to everyone later.

Thoughts of Mark, knives, and Indians bubbled in his mind like beans in a kettle. Then he heard a distant rumbling.

"What's that?" Ruthie asked.

Suddenly Pa appeared and motioned them inside the wagon. "Buffalo stampede," he explained. "They're headed toward us. Get in here quick!"

Luke's mouth went dry. He sensed danger. Pa never let them ride in the wagon. He said it would tire the oxen. Luke looked back and saw Jake driving the Smiths'

wagon. Mazie peeked from inside the flap.

Ma sat on the driver's seat of their wagon holding the reins. Pa grabbed his rifle and joined her as the rumbling grew to a roar. The earth shook beneath the wagon wheels. Luke peeked out the flap. The buffalo looked like a sea of brown flowing toward them.

But waves didn't snort and bellow. One critter ran so close, Luke saw its yellowish eyes. He choked on dust. Grit coated his teeth and tongue. The wagons couldn't turn these critters back. Luke wanted to hide, but he couldn't bear not to look.

Suddenly rifle shots rang from every wagon. At first, the buffalo kept coming. Then two fell. A moment later, three more collapsed.

"They're turning!" Pa shouted.

The men fired until the herd changed direction. After the danger had passed, Jake stopped the wagon train. Men ran to butcher the fallen animals.

"Take only enough meat for two meals," Jake ordered. "Extra weight could stall us in the mountains."

The men obeyed. As the wagon train pulled away, a group of Indians galloped up on ponies. Luke shuddered. The dozen Indians had appeared out of nowhere.

"We're safe," Pa said. "They only want fresh meat."

Everyone enjoyed grilled buffalo for supper and breakfast. Then they faced the mountains. Luke had never seen a trail so steep and narrow. Breathing came hard for both people and oxen.

Hairpin turns in the trail curved sharply. Luke and Ruthie clung to the wagon as they walked. Then Luke peered over the trail's edge. Cold sweat slicked his hands. His head swam, and he lost his grip. His feet slipped off the trail.

Chapter 6

Heart and Soul

Rocks tumbled from the path, but Luke never heard them land. Ruthie grabbed his shirttail. Pa leaned down and yanked him back onto the trail. Ma helped him into the wagon.

"Easy, Luke," Pa said, panting.

Tears stung Luke's eyelids, but he blinked them back. He'd almost fallen. He'd needed Ruthie and Pa to rescue him. He was as ashamed as he was scared. Ma sobbed as she hugged him.

"It was the **altitude**, Luke," Pa said. "Even strong men get woozy in thin mountain air."

Luke stuck his head through the canvas opening. He tossed his breakfast onto the trail. The vomiting weakened him. He slept in the wagon while the family continued walking up the trail.

It took days to travel through the mountains. Ma's **sassafras** tea soothed Luke's stomach. At last, Luke felt strong and fit.

Many of the oxen didn't survive the steep journey up the mountain. When the wagon train finally reached level ground, Ruthie cried for all the lost animals. Ma didn't cry until Blue and Red began to slow down.

"What's wrong with the oxen, Pa?" Luke asked.

Pioneers often had to lighten their loads by leaving items behind along the trail.

"They're purely tired out," Pa said. "They've been pulling their load for four months. They need grain and water, but there isn't any nearby."

"They need a lighter load," Ma said. "Let's leave some things behind."

Luke remembered seeing chairs and tables scattered along the trail. "What should we leave?" he asked.

"We'll start with the heavy box of Grandma's china," Ma said. "Then my rocking chair."

Ruthie left her dolls against a **sapling**. Luke hid his games and ice skates under some brush.

"Maybe we'll come back for them later," Luke said. But he knew they wouldn't.

"The rug and tool box can go," Pa said, "but save our tools. We need them."

They left behind many prized possessions. Nobody cried—at least not when the others could see.

Later they stopped at the steep path down to the Snake River. Now they welcomed their lighter load as they roped the wagon and set it beside the river.

"Can we make it across the water?" Luke asked.

Crossing bodies of water was one of the most difficult and dangerous parts of the trail.

"We have to," Pa said. "Jake says we'll chain our wagons together and hitch several ox teams to them. Their united strength will pull the wagons through the swift current. Let's start stuffing clothes into the wagon cracks."

"Why?" Luke asked.

"To keep the water out," Pa said. "I've already tarred some cracks. We'll make it."

Luke tried to believe Pa. Oxen snorted. Wagons groaned. They eased into the river a few wagons at a time. Sometimes water barely rippled over the wheel rims. Other times it lapped at the wagon bed.

Ruthie didn't scream when she slipped and fell. Only Luke heard the quiet splash.

"Float with the current!" Luke shouted. He sprinted along the shore, found a willow branch, and splashed into the water. The strong current sucked at his legs. He eased closer to Ruthie and held out the branch to her. He kept a firm grip on the other end.

"Grab hold, Ruthie. Grab it."

Ruthie caught the branch and held on.

"Let me help," Mazie said, splashing toward Luke. She grabbed Luke's hand to steady him and give him strength. They dug their heels into the river rocks.

Then Jake saw their plight. He rode Hawkeye into the river. Leaning low, he swooped Ruthie up and carried her to the other side. Then he returned for Mazie and Luke.

Hours passed before all the wagons crossed the river.

"Thanks, Luke," Ruthie said later when they were getting warm around a campfire. "You saved my life."

31

"Sure," Luke said, blushing. "Mazie, Jake, and Hawkeye helped. Sometimes brave deeds take a heap of backup folks."

— · — · — · — · — · — · — · —

Luke began to hate the endless trail. They'd lost many of their possessions. The oxen had grown rail thin.

But everyone was alive. That was the important thing.

Nobody talked much anymore. Even Mazie had stopped singing at campfire. Then one day, Peter Lee rode up.

"We're here!" he yelled. "We've arrived in Oregon! We've conquered over two thousand miles."

Even the oxen found new strength. They pulled the wagon train to a hilltop. Everyone looked down at the green valley below.

"There's our new home!" Pa shouted.

Luke inhaled the fragrance of fir trees. He stood silently, awed by the lush grass and wildflowers. Which part of this beauty belonged to the Fletchers? He knew Pa would decide that later. Right now, he was just feeling glad to have survived the journey.

Inner voices no longer shouted *coward*. Somewhere along the trail, he'd lost his fear—or maybe he'd just faced it and won.

Whether they called themselves emigrants or pioneers, determination had made them all brave. Now they would help form the heart and soul of Oregon.

Luke wished Mark could see them now. But then again, maybe he could. Either way, Luke knew that his brother would be with them in spirit as they built their new life here on the Oregon prairie.

Oregon Fever

Jobs were scarce in America in the early 1840s. Fur traders and adventurers sometimes passed through the Midwest. They told tales of Oregon's riches. Poor families wanting better lives began heading west.

These families called themselves emigrants. Oregon was not a state yet. The emigrants were traveling to a foreign land. Pioneers were people traveling in their own country to settle new lands. Once Oregon became a state, some settlers called themselves *pioneers*.

The emigrants left from the banks of the Missouri River. Families took horses and cows. They packed all other possessions in covered wagons. Sometimes they took chickens in cages attached to their wagons.

The small wagons were narrow and about 14 feet long. Hoops over the wagon bed supported the cover, which was usually a thick, oiled cotton. The wagons rolled on huge iron-covered wheels. A team of four to six oxen pulled this heavy load.

and pieces of furniture. Riding space was tight. One person sat on the driver's seat to guide the oxen. Babies rode in cradles. Other family members walked.

The 2000-mile trip to Oregon took about 4–6 months. Wagon trains traveled the Oregon Trail for over 25 years. More than 400,000 people made the hard journey. Many people who started the trip did not survive.

Emigrants often painted their wagons **patriotic** colors. Red wheels, white covers, and blue wagon beds were common along the trail.

The wagons carried food, tools, bedding, and a few clothes

Traveling together provided some protection for wagon trains. Still, many dangers awaited the emigrants.

Hostile Indians sometimes attacked and killed the travelers. But many Indians were friendly. They shared their food and showed emigrants where to find game. They helped repair wagons. Emigrants sometimes paid Indians for help in crossing rivers.

Illness claimed many lives on the Oregon Trail. Many emigrants died of cholera. At the time, people didn't know that drinking impure water could cause diseases.

Travelers also died from accidents and drownings at river crossings. Others suffered from the effects of the high mountain altitudes.

One man was paid to take charge of each wagon train. This wagon master decided who could go on the trip. He also made the rules.

The wagon master worked with a scout who rode ahead of the train. The scout would return with news of the trail ahead.

The wagon master established the train's routine. The group

Monuments were built for victims of the Oregon Trail.

usually traveled six days a week. The wagons stopped late in the afternoon. Eight or more wagons then formed circles.

Space inside the circles provided protection from Indians and wolves. It gave oxen a place to graze. Families raised sleeping tents and made campfires within the circles.

Everyone did daily chores. Men tended to the oxen and kept the wagon in good condition. Women prepared the meals and cared for the children. Children gathered wood or buffalo dung for the campfires. They also shook out the bedding and carried water.

The first half of the trip passed over many flat prairies. Travelers saw unusual sights. Some hiked off the trail for close-up views of outcroppings. They saw Chimney Rock, Jail Rock, and Courthouse Rock. Scott's Bluff, a steep cliff rising to 700 feet, was also a popular attraction.

The wagons stopped briefly at Fort Kearney and Fort Laramie in Nebraska territory. There, travelers could rest and buy supplies. Then they faced the second half of the trail, where travel became more difficult.

Thousands of pioneers carved their names into the soft sandstone of Register Cliff.

Devils Gate

Chimney Rock

Trail's End

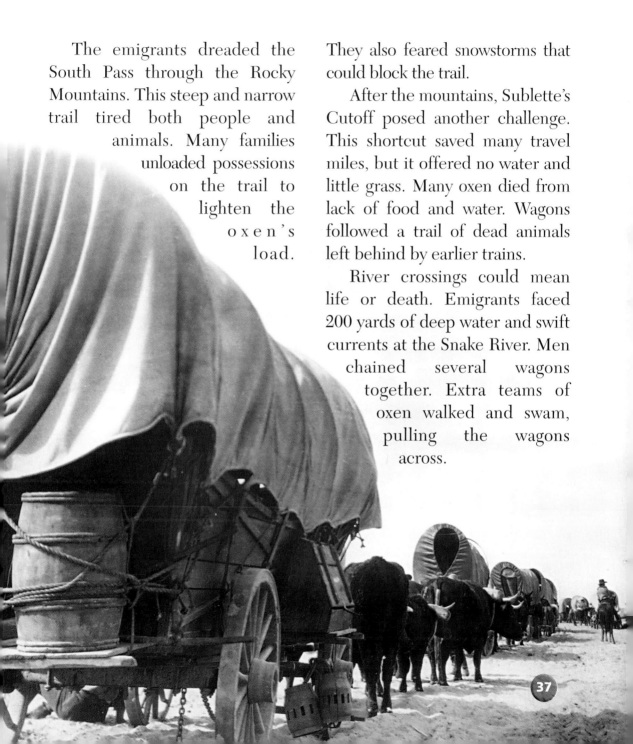

The emigrants dreaded the South Pass through the Rocky Mountains. This steep and narrow trail tired both people and animals. Many families unloaded possessions on the trail to lighten the oxen's load.

They also feared snowstorms that could block the trail.

After the mountains, Sublette's Cutoff posed another challenge. This shortcut saved many travel miles, but it offered no water and little grass. Many oxen died from lack of food and water. Wagons followed a trail of dead animals left behind by earlier trains.

River crossings could mean life or death. Emigrants faced 200 yards of deep water and swift currents at the Snake River. Men chained several wagons together. Extra teams of oxen walked and swam, pulling the wagons across.

Weary emigrants could cross rivers by ferry. But ferrymen charged high fares—sometimes as much as the price of an ox. And sometimes overloaded ferryboats sank.

Another hundred miles brought the travelers to Fort Boise. There, they rested. They prepared to cross the Blue Mountains and then the Columbia River. Finally the travelers reached the end of the trail at Fort Vancouver.

Near the fort lay the beautiful Willamette Valley. It was the travelers' dream come true—the dream that had kept them going for so many months.

At the end of the journey, one emigrant wrote, "We lost everything but our lives." Many lost everything, *including* their lives.

Willamette Valley

Survivors spread out to establish farms and small towns. Oregon grew. Small towns became cities. Frame houses replaced log cabins.

Eventually Oregon began to look like the land the emigrants had left behind. They called it home.

To follow the Oregon Trail online, visit the following Web sites.

http://www.pbs.org/opb/oregontrail/

Learn interesting facts, myths, and trivia at this informational site.

http://www.endoftheoregontrail.org

Become an Oregon Trail expert by investigating the trail's history, viewing a detailed diagram and description of prairie schooners, and checking out provisions and prices of the time.

http://www.ku.edu/kansas/seneca/oregon

This site provides a thorough look at the Oregon Trail as well as several other pioneer trails in the United States.

http://www.isu.edu/~trinmich/Sites.html

Visit the historic sites along the Oregon Trail, including Courthouse Rock, Chimney Rock, Fort Laramie, Fort Kearney, and Fort Vancouver.

Glossary

adobe bricks made of dried straw and clay

altitude height above sea level

Appaloosa rugged saddle horse usually having a white or solid-colored coat with small spots

bank rising land or steep slope bordering a body of water

branding iron heated metal tool used to mark animals to show ownership

broke packed up gear and left a campsite

buckskin horse of a light yellowish brown color with a black mane and tail

calico cotton fabric

cholera disease that affects the stomach

dung waste material from an animal

emigrant person who leaves a country to settle in another area

foreign relating to a country other than one's own

four-poster bed bed with tall posts in each corner

game animals hunted for food or sport

outcropping rock formation that sticks out of the ground

patriotic inspired by love of one's country

prairie schooner covered wagon

sapling young tree

sassafras tree with leaves that can be brewed for tea

scouting exploring an area to look for food, shelter, or enemies

thong strip of leather or animal hide (skin)

tom-tom long, narrow drum

tongue structure with an indentation that fits into another piece

wagon train group of wagons that traveled together